Love Language

ALLEN E. FIELDS

ISBN: 979-8-218-39607-7

First Edition

Printed in the U.S.A.

Published by Poets Pantry Publishing
Bronx, New York

ACKNOWLEDGMENTS

Without God, this book would not have been possible. I extend my heartfelt gratitude to the wonderful individuals who have played pivotal roles in my life. First and foremost, a special thank you to my dear grandmother, Mary Ann (may she rest in peace), my mother, Helen, and my sister, Brandi. To my cherished daughters, Asia, Faith, and Janay, along with my niece, Tori, and nephew, Trayshawn, your unwavering love and support mean the world to me.

I also want to express my appreciation for the constant encouragement from my aunts (Bunnie, Susan, Pia, Faith, Jayne, Roxane), uncles (Mickey, may he rest in peace, Pepe, Barry, may he rest in peace, Mitchell, Paul, Rodney), and a multitude of cousins.

To Rob, CP, and Kennard, your enduring friendships are truly invaluable. A special acknowledgment goes to Staci and Traci, whom I consider my extended sisters and trusted sounding boards. To my friends, watching you strive for your goals and dreams have kept me motivated.

I'd like to give a heartfelt shoutout to Michelle K for believing in my work right from the beginning. Lastly, a profound thank you to Tracé Wilkins Francis, who helped me birth this book. Thank you for taking a chance on me.

I appreciate you all. Nothing but love.

TABLE OF CONTENTS

Receive Me

I'm not here to create chaos in your life
or make it a mess.
My goal is to help you lessen your stress.
I won't hide from you and will open my heart.
I'll become your comfort zone by doing my part.
I'll be giving you joy and simple satisfaction.
It's easy to say, so I'll back it with my actions
All you want is the truth and your mind at ease,
someone who can ignite your imagination
and a stimulating tease.
You are far from a lost cause that I can see.
You only want emotional stability
and the ability to be mentally free.
I only ask that you give me a fair chance.
My goal is to be your best and last dance.

All About Us

We've done this dance without any fuss.

It's time we change the you and I to us.

I come to you and ask for your hand.

Will you allow me the pleasure of being your man?

Will you accept all my flaws as they have come to be?

Will you go through the ups and downs

while being there for me?

I want to be there for you, and that's no lie.

I'll keep you safe, even if it meant I would die.

What I feel for you can't be wrong.

Patience is a virtue, and it's been too long.

This has been on my mind,

so can we discuss it now?

Your happiness is my priority,

and you won't have to show me how.

As One

Having you come into my life has been
a blessing in disguise.
Getting to know you was better than I could
have ever dreamed or thought to surmise.
Behind every successful man, there is a strong
and supportive woman.
Being friends first made the transition easy for me.
I saw all the traits I needed to see.
You've helped me see the world so clear and bright.
Where there was once darkness, there is now light.
I've shared my most personal secrets with you
because it's all about trust.
Some thoughts were so deep within me,
that telling you was a must.
My wings are spread, and you've allowed my soul
to be free.
I've revealed my heart to you, so will you take
this journey with me?

Everything To Me

From the first day we met, I could see it in your eyes.
They told me you were beyond tired of the lies.
From that moment on, only one mission
was on my mind.
I could not stop envisioning you as my beautiful bride.
I want to give you everything, from the moon to the
stars in the universe.
I hope you know how appreciative I am of all that
you're worth.
Still though, the moon and stars wouldn't even
be enough, you see,
To show you how much you mean to me.
Thank you for including me in your plans,
and for helping me to become an even better man
Dreams do come true,
and I'll leave you with this.
I'm ever grateful for you,
The angel I get to fall in love with.

Dream of A Woman's Nourishment

I want to be the reason your heart skips a beat,
the one to sweep you off your feet.
I want to be the one who shares that spliff,
the one you want to fulfill your fantasies with.
I want to be the one you let deep inside,
the one who's name you say with pride.
I want to be the one you always miss,
the one you want to passionately kiss.
I want to be the one who helps you forget your past,
the one you want to be your last.

Blessed

Where I was suffocating,

I can now breathe with you.

Where there was darkness,

you are now a light to reveal all that's true.

Where I felt so much pain,

you have showed me how much love

between us does remain.

Where I was lost and could not find my way,

you gave me a reason to face the next day.

Where I felt isolated and alone,

you opened my mind and heart to atone.

Where I never thought I would find that passion

in my life,

God sent you and presented the opportunity

to be my wife.

Where I was frustrated and stressed,

you are now beside me to make me feel most blessed.

Recipe For Love

People often wonder what are the ingredients for love,

but the answer to that question starts up above.

Pay close attention, so you don't miss.

I've come to see it reads just like a grocery list.

The foundation starts with friendship and trust,

leading to changing you and I to US.

Next, is honesty, let it rise above all.

Lies are the enemy, causing pillars to fall.

Follow and listen to your heart, for it will lead the way,

steering you in the right direction and clear words to say.

Communication is a must, so be sure to talk it out.

Do so in a caring manner, remembering never to shout.

Add some passion, and give it everything you got.

Leave nothing to chance, and you'll find that ideal spot.

I See You

To hear your voice is total bliss.

I'm already imagining our first kiss.

The vibe and connection we share grew so fast.

You are a welcome difference from those in my past.

Time has no say in what I'm feeling.

The possibilities are endless, an open ceiling.

I want it all: your mind, body, and soul.

After that, we'll go down the rabbit hole.

All I need is your permission to access the front door.

You have no idea how each day

I crave your presence more and more.

Destiny

All my life, I've patiently waited for her to cross my path.

With my eyes wide open, as it happens,

it will all add up like simple math.

You can not hesitate, or you will miss your chance.

Approach her with confidence, and let her know your

intentions in advance.

Listen to her stories, and embrace her relationships

of the past.

Although you were not her first love,

show her you will be her last.

This situation is critical and a once in a lifetime

opportunity.

I have complete control of my destiny.

Joy

It's not enough for me to only put a smile on your face.

I desire to make you feel comfortable,

giving you an emotional safe place.

The goal is to satisfy you on every level,

no matter how long it takes.

Getting to know you is the key,

being open and honest, never fake.

Giving you pleasure consumes my mind,

searching for those deep stimulations

that I want to find.

I want to make those past disappointments a thing

of the past.

Stability, security, and love are what makes

a relationship last.

What you bring to the table makes my dreams come true,

but my greatest joy comes when you finally say I do.

Your Kiss

I love the feel of your sensual lips.

I'm wanting to take your breath away.

What a way to start and end the day.

It surely lures me in, making me want to stay.

It's easy to see why I care for you so much,

from your kind heart and your intellect

to your soft touch.

When I first saw the fullness of them,

I fantasized about their taste.

Earning that privilege,

I put my emotions into it with no time to waste.

When it finally happened, it was everything I expected.

Now I crave your kiss just as I suspected.

Blissful Abyss

Being with the ideal woman can feel like a distant
memory trapped in a dream.
Finding her among a nightmare reality is possible
to form a dynamic team.
You have to stay positive through all the hurt and pain.
Remember that sunshine always follows the rain.
Keep negative thoughts out of your mind,
even in a mess.
Staying focused and optimistic is the key to success
When you meet her, the picture will become very clear.
Now it's time to get to work; No time for fear.
Show her you are serious with actions that are true.
It's all worth it in the end because the prize is you.

Love Affair

I crave your mind, body, and soul.

Where there was emptiness,

you have since filled that hole.

You carry yourself with such grace,

makes me want to spend time with you and share

the same intimate space.

I recognize you have a lot to offer and never flaunt,

choosing you was easy because you are what I want.

There is nothing to think about; my heart is set.

I am convinced my happiness is with you, a sure bet.

With you, there is no one who can compare.

I yearn to begin a forever with you, a forever love affair.

Realistic Fantasy

Coming across you was unexpected and by happenstance.
You coming into my life was not by chance.
From the very start,
I could tell being with you would be the best part.
The way you touched my soul was frightening.
I was focused on me, myself, and I before being struck
by your lightning.
I miss gazing into your eyes,
mesmerized by its depth and limitlessness like the sky.
In a short amount of time,
you stole my heart, and that was fine.
I can stare at you for hours on end.
I knew I wanted to be more than a friend.
Opening up to you was easy because you made it
that way.
I was free to be me, including honest words to say.
You continue to inspire me to reach for the stars,
never to restrict my dreams that expand far.
Spending time with you only confirmed
what I felt inside.

It was definitely love because my sight was very clear
and not blind.
You must understand that you are beautiful,
and I'm attracted to your size.
It's your mind, heart, and love that is really
the ultimate prize.

Utopia Exists

Utopia exists because it lives within your heart and mind.

Don't let anyone tell you different

just because it's something they don't believe

or can't find.

The communication will be so open and honest,

we will come to have a very good understanding

of each other.

We'll be free from constraints and any attempts

to smother.

She will make me feel strong enough to freely share

and express my emotions,

never judging me with any terrible preconceived notions.

She will create a space safe enough for me

to be unapologetically vulnerable.

She will hug my soul making me nothing

less than comfortable.

She will follow all these hugs up with plenty of love

and affection,

so this would be the norm, not the exception.

I will be allowed to be myself without fear

of having that information be weaponized

against me at a later time;

the happiness will grow deep in me as my aura shines.

She will make it a priority to tell me my presence

is wanted,

while allowing me to be the man she envisioned to see.

Now I can flourish as the protector,

provider and provisioner I was meant to be.

Fascinated

I often wondered if you were a dream,

I have to pinch myself to realize we are a team.

I'm hypnotized by the sound of your voice,

still amazed by the fact that I was your choice.

I find your beauty mesmerizing, that's why I stare,

I can spend hours making you blush without a care.

Your smile illuminates the dark,

I was fascinated beyond belief, falling for you hard.

It is my hope that you know,

you're in possession of my heart.

Mission Possible

Stay with me.

There is a method to my madness, and it's not a game,

I'm trying to get your attention and ask you your name.

The thoughts in my mind can seem chaotic,

but as I look into your eyes,

they calm me because they're so hypnotic.

Every day I get closer to the goal I want to achieve.

Nothing will deter my effort,

and I must continue to believe.

You take your time to see me clearly and find out

what I'm all about.

As our conversation intensifies, you always get

your point across and never need to shout.

The task can seem daunting,

and the process may be difficult.

The foundation formed has to be solidly built.

Be consistent in appreciating her, knowing her worth.

Acknowledging her value, that's logical,

No matter the obstacles, being with you is still possible.

My Chance

I asked God to send me a woman who is real and true,

but when we first met, I had no idea it could be you.

As I got to know the person you are,

it was clear to me the many lovely possibilities

for exploration of new horizons near and far.

I knew that putting my time, energy,

and effort into you would be worth it.

Everything you bring to the table makes you

the closest thing I've ever had to perfect.

After getting a taste of your affection and vibe,

I yearned to know more,

even the deepest parts you try to hide.

The journey has just begun, and I treasure each day.

Earning and maintaining your trust is my top priority,

so it's vital I do what I say.

Ready For You

I'm not here to sell you a false dream.

I only want to be a part of your life,

earn and keep my part on your team.

I come in peace; this is not a scam.

I approach you humbly and with respect because

this is who I am.

The goal is to be a positive addition to your life,

to show you how serious I am,

ultimately choosing to be my wife.

Don't be fooled; I'm not arrogant.

I know my worth and value, I'm just confident.

It's not just you who is willing to submit.

I'm more than eager to fully give myself

and sincerely commit.

Accept Me

Make no mistake; I want you in the worst way.

Forget the drama and games;

I'm ready to give you what you desire every day.

I want nothing more than to add peace in your space,

so please let me in love's door.

I understand making you happy is a must.

Same applies for proving to you I can be the one you trust.

Your soul will be ignited and it will be evident by

the expression on your face.

I want others to wonder where is your happy destination,

It's simply mental, emotional, and physical stimulation.

This Opportunity Nourishes Inspiration

Let me tell you about this woman I know.

She is authentic, and nothing she does is for show.

She is raw with emotion and not afraid to care.

She radiates positive energy that you would

certainly want to get close enough to share.

She tells me stories,

not knowing I've been through the same.

It's like she knows where to find me in the dark

without saying my name.

The way in which she chooses to communicate,

Her words grabs ahold of my soul, so this can't be fake.

Every day I wake up with her on my mind.

I can't let her go because she is a rare find.

We immediately connected,

and there was definitely a sensual vibe.

We have embarked on this journey, a beautiful drive.

I can't lie. The depth of her beauty is within her eyes.

I yearn to feel her thick thighs.

To know her is to be comforted by a blanket,

so soft and warm.

Amongst all the chaos around you,

she will be your peace within the storm.

With her, it's way more than sex.

She is like a mystery book I can't put down filled

with interesting text.

I've told you enough, now it's time to go,

Just wanted to tell you about this magnificent woman

I know.

The Truth

You are becoming the air I breathe,

the calm in a storm or rough seas.

You are what's most important to me.

In the darkness, you are the only one I see.

I will be patient with you because

it's only a matter of time.

I strive more and more every day to make you mine.

If you were never sure about us or had any doubt,

I want you to know how I feel and understand

what my intentions are about.

Let me be very clear.

You're already such an irreplaceable part of my life.

My end goal is to put a ring on your finger

and make you my wife.

It Is

What is it?
It's a dream that won't go away,
a daydream that let's your mind play.

Who is it?
There is no rhyme or reason; it's just how you feel.
It has the power to inspire and even heal.

Why is it?
Searching for an answer you always wanted to know,
it has unlocked your soul, allowing your aura to glow.

When is it?
You never see it coming, not sure what to expect.
Just acknowledge its presence and show
the proper respect.

How is it?
Never challenge what only God can see.
Fully accept and embrace the blessing, let it be.

An Idea

Stop wasting minutes on things
that don't make you think.
Time waits for nobody. You'll miss it if you blink.
We should all crave stimulating conversation
for the mind.
It will light up brain cells and tickle the spine.
Deep in thought about events in the past,
those surviving memories will certainly last.
Now sit back and ponder, what is there to do?
Before you utter a word, think it through.

Why Not Me?

It's been a long time coming, so I hope this is not a dream.

My aura is running wild, like a fast moving stream.

I embrace this feeling with all my heart.

I promise to give my all and do my part.

I'm not afraid to open up and allow my heart to receive.

I always had faith and had to believe.

Thank you God for opening my eyes to see.

I won't fight this feeling, and let it be.

That four letter gift was sent from above.

The sign was there all along as a beautiful dove.

A Dreamed Reality

Despite everything she has been through,

the ups and downs, the success and failures,

the heartbreaks, and the loss of loved ones,

she is not only still standing but thriving and improving.

Don't doubt her.

To underestimate her would be a mistake.

Expectations don't scare her.

Nobody will be as hard on her as she is on herself.

She is motivated, driven, and has a clear plan and focus

to obtain her goals.

She will not be distracted by shiny objects.

She doesn't have time to waste.

She believes in herself and is all in.

She understands that she cannot do it alone,

but only a select few will get to experience the journey.

Those select few will be those who can offer

something positive to the process.

Resistance and obstacles will not slow her down
or stop her.
She will learn, adapt and overcome.
She is on her grind every day and has no time
to play games.
It can't be all business, so some fun is sprinkled
in to keep her sane.

Absolutely beautiful inside and out.
A humble soul and a quiet aura.
Her smile can move mountains.
Her eyes can hypnotize your spirit.
Her touch can reach your heart.
Her kiss will take your breath away.
All I need is her permission.

Got You

Let me introduce myself properly to you.

I am your future. I sense your skepticism, but it's true.

I admire you because you handle your own.

I'm looking for a queen to compliment my throne.

I'm not here to interrupt your flow.

Let's get together and produce our life's show.

I see you out there grinding, always on your hustle;

I promise I'm not here to waste your time.

I don't want to stop your shine,

just want to match your vibe.

I can tell by looking in your eyes what you really feel

You're tired of having to control everything and ready

to let go of the wheel.

You are ready to sit back and bask in your femininity.

Time to sit in the passenger seat.

Hand me those keys.

Can You Hear Me?

To my future wife,

I am writing you so you fully understand the scope of my intentions. I love you because you are everything I asked God for. You are kind, warm hearted, patient, humble, ambitious, and a nurturer. The way you talk to me is so uplifting. You motivate me to be the best man I can be. Your touch is so comforting, I feel I don't have a worry in the world. Your kiss reaches my heart with happiness. Your love engulfs my soul like a warm blanket. Our communication is unpretentious and honest. It has become a daily necessity. I crave all of you, quirks and imperfections included, and I will give you all of me in return. My world is a better place with you in it. With you at my side, nothing is impossible. You see me like no other, and I could never hide from you. You are my eternity.

With endless passion,

Your future husband

Desire

Nothing worth having is easy.

You are worth EVERYTHING I have to give.

I want to experience you like no one else.

I want to ultimately start OUR journey.

Our lives have been good separately,

but why can't we be EXCEPTIONAL together?

I only want that with you.

Beautiful Struggle

When I look at you, a calmness comes over me,

then the excitement hits me with what I see.

It's an internal chaos you couldn't understand.

Just know I desire to be your man.

It's a beautiful struggle, and I will never complain.

My cravings for you burn like a never-ending flame.

I will always express my feelings to you

without involving my ego.

It's necessary to avoid confusion,

thus making our connection better flow.

Nothing worth having is easy,

so I plan to give efforts that are my very best.

The passion in me connects to the purpose in you,

unlike any connection with all the rest.

Are You Her?

I am in search of her, the one who will set my heart free.

Her image in my dreams are so real,

even a blind man can see.

Not just anyone will do;

the task is too important to leave it up to chance.

I will not waver on what I believe;

nothing will make me on my stance.

The path to my relationship bliss is about patience

and understanding,

waiting for a sign, never in a rush or being demanding.

Make yourself known; show me in plain sight.

I promise to love you eternally

like the stars across the sky during an everlasting

moonlit night.

Lots Of Lovin

My mission is to be with you.

For your love, nothing will stop me from doing all

that I need to do.

Your skin shines like the sands of an oasis.

My mind wanders to many seductive places.

Some say the blacker the berry, the sweeter the juice.

When we get together, only intimacy will follow

the passion you and I will produce.

Understand I crave your love in order to feed

my heart's hunger.

Your sweet, fulfilling touch is like the lightning

to all my thunder.

My heart yearns to give you everything within me.

I'm an open book; my aura is there for you to see.

Stay Ready

I'm focused on my goals and purpose.

The grind is real, and the ideal relationship

is just under the surface.

Even if I slip, I won't fail,

Your love is far too valuable to ever be on sale.

Whatever the cost is, I'll pay,

You are everything I want, so I pray.

Life can be chaotic with many thunderous skies.

I will not miss my opportunity to love you.

That's no lie.

No matter how much you try to avoid with speed,

you will see I'm not only a want,

but exactly what you need.

Unchained Passion

Love is an intense feeling, but who to love is,
in some ways, a choice.
It's up to you to make the right decision,
so follow your inner voice.
Stop waiting for the perfect partner.
You control the narrative of your book,
and you alone, are the author.
Trust yourself, and never second guess.
Stand on principle, and be reasonable.
You will pass the mental and spiritual test.
Once you find that emotional connection,
nurture it with maximum affection.
Only then can you reach the ultimate relationship goal,
a healthy, peaceful journey being in a truly loving role.

www.ingramcontent.com/pod-product-compliance
Lightning Source LLC
Chambersburg PA
CBHW040844010826
48978CB00012BB/889